Anonymous

Premature Death

its promotion or prevention

Anonymous

Premature Death
its promotion or prevention

ISBN/EAN: 9783337403874

Printed in Europe, USA, Canada, Australia, Japan

Cover: Foto ©Andreas Hilbeck / pixelio.de

More available books at **www.hansebooks.com**

HEALTH PRIMERS.

PREMATURE DEATH:

ITS

PROMOTION OR PREVENTION.

NEW YORK:

D. APPLETON AND COMPANY,

549 & 551 BROADWAY.

1879.

CONTENTS.

———◆◇◆———

	PAGE
THE RUDIMENTARY ARITHMETIC OF PREMATURE DEATH	5
THE CAUSES OF PREMATURE DEATH	7
THE CONDITIONS UNDER WHICH THE CAUSES OF PREMATURE DEATH OPERATE	14
THE PREVENTION OF PREMATURE DEATH	69

PREMATURE DEATH:

ITS PROMOTION OR PREVENTION.

CHAPTER I.

THE RUDIMENTARY ARITHMETIC OF PREMATURE DEATH.

OF the twenty-five millions (25,000,000) of people who form the population of England and Wales, half a million or thereabout (500,000) die, on the average, every year.

Of these deaths *one-tenth* only (50,000) are of persons who have reached the full term of life, namely, seventy-five years and upwards; *nine-tenths* are *premature*, that is to say, are deaths of persons whose lives have been cut short before the expiration of their natural term.

Somewhat less than *one-fourth* of the 450,000 persons who every year die prematurely (24 per cent. = 108,000) die in infancy; somewhat over *four-tenths* (41 per cent. = 184,500), including those who die in infancy, die by the time the fifth year of life is completed; the deaths of the remaining *six-tenths* nearly (59 per cent. = 266,000) are distributed pretty equally over the period of life between childhood and old age.

Premature death, as here considered, comprehends all deaths except deaths from old age. The distinction is not a mere verbal redundancy. It marks a point of view from which the contemplation of death is best approached for the purposes of health preservation whether in its public or its private aspects. A just sense of the gravity and scope of the questions involved in the advancement of the health, whether of a community, or of a household, or of an individual, is in the main dependent upon the accuracy of our conceptions as to the *prematureness* of the vastly greater number of the deaths which occur among a population.

The foundation of *preventive medicine*—or, as it is termed in its more familiarly known aspect, *sanitary science*—rests on our knowledge of the causes of this excessive amount of premature death, of the conditions under which these causes operate, and of the extent to which they are avoidable.

CHAPTER II.

THE CAUSES OF PREMATURE DEATH.

And first of the *causes* of premature death :—

The foremost place among these is held by *diseases of the lungs*, including *phthisis*—the *consumption* of popular language. More than *one-fourth* (26 per cent. = 130,000) of the whole number of premature deaths are caused by this class of diseases.

Next in order of predominance are the *infectious diseases*—the eruptive, contagious, or infectious fevers, small-pox, scarlet fever, measles, typhus, enteric (typhoid) fever, &c. These cause nearly a *sixth* (15·5 per cent. = 78,700) of the premature deaths.

Then, occupying the third place among the causes of death, come the *diseases of the brain and nervous system*, including *hydrocephalus*. These give rise to about an *eighth* of the premature deaths (12 per cent. = 54,000).

The fourth place is taken by certain diseases classified along with the infectious diseases as *general* maladies, the whole system being affected by them as a direct result of their development and progress, and not as a secondary consequence of the local disturbance of particular organs. The diseases referred to, here for convenience considered apart, include rheumatism, gout, syphilis, cancer, scrofula in certain forms, purples, scurvy, privation, alcoholic poisoning (alcoholism), &c., and cause a *tenth* of the premature deaths (10 per cent. = 45,000).

Fifth in order of magnitude are the *developmental diseases*, so called (exclusive of old age), namely premature birth, teething, childbed, atrophy and debility, &c. These cause an *eleventh* of the premature deaths (9 per cent. = 40,500).

Sixth are the *diseases of the heart and blood-vessels*, including dropsy (6 per cent. = 30,000) :

Seventh, the diseases of the *stomach, intestines, and associated organs* (4 per cent. = 20,000) :

Eighth, the results of *violence*, including suicide (3 per cent. = 15,000) :

Ninth, the diseases of the kidney and urinary organs (1·5 per cent. = 6750) :

Finally follow in succession (each forming 1 per cent. or under of the whole mortality) *diseases of the joints* and *diseases of the skin*.

Such is a general statement of the causes of premature death given in the order of their relative importance. If now the particular diseases which are most fatal in the several classes are set forth in the order of their mortality, taking for this purpose certain calculations of the Registrar-General for the twenty-five years 1850–74,* the following result is obtained :—

CLASS I.—*Diseases of Lungs, &c.*

	Annual Mortality to 1,000,000 during 25 years 1850–74.
Phthisis	2567·2
Bronchitis	1596·5
Pneumonia	1163·1
Other lung diseases	512·4

CLASS II.—*Infectious Diseases.*

Scarlet-fever and Diphtheria†	1038·0
Continued fevers (Typhus, Enteric fever, &c.)	866·2
Whooping-cough	514·0
Measles	428·0
Small-pox	250·0
Erysipelas	97·0
[Malignant cholera	81·0]
Other infectious diseases.	206·0

CLASS III.—*Diseases of the Brain and Nervous System.*

Convulsions	1265·8
Paralysis	486·0
Apoplexy	477·0
Hydrocephalus	370·0
Other brain diseases, &c.	577·5

* The 37th Annual Report of Registrar-General, p. 237.
† Diphtheria was not distinguished from scarlet-fever in the Registers for much of this period.

CLASS IV.—*General Diseases, &c.*

Cancer	309·0
Wasting (mesenteric) of infants	282·0
Croup	240·0
Scrofula	142·0
Rheumatism	109·0
Other general diseases	39·4

CLASS V.—*Developmental Diseases* (exclusive of Old Age).

Atrophy and Debility	1191·4
Premature birth	604·9
Teething	206·6
Childbirth	112·0
Other developmental diseases	62·9

CLASS VI.—*Diseases of the Heart, &c.*

Heart diseases, &c.	949·7

CLASS VII.—*Diseases of the Digestive Organs.*

Diarrhœa (890·0)	
[Simple Cholera (38·0)]	995·2
Dysentery (67·2)	
Liver disease	238·0
Inflammation of the bowels (Enteritis) . .	162·0
Stomach diseases, &c.	128·0
Other diseases of digestive organs	477·0

CLASS VIII.—*Violent Deaths.*

Accident, homicide, suicide	761·3

CLASS IX.—*Diseases of Urinary Organs.*

Kidney disease, &c.	272·3

CLASS X.—*Diseases of Joints.*

Joint disease . . . . 77·4

CLASS XI.—*Diseases of Skin.*

Skin disease . . . . 57·0

The foregoing data show the relative importance of the different classes of disease as causes of premature death, and of the particular diseases giving rise to the greatest mortality in the larger number of the classes. The data are given as to the classes of disease with reference to the population at all ages under seventy-five years ; and as to particular diseases, with reference to the population at all ages, as if the mortality from the various diseases were distributed equally among the people within the period of life designated. It must now be understood that the mortality from the several diseases and classes of disease falls with very different force at various periods of life. There is a wide difference between the incidence of the several causes of death in infancy, in childhood, in youth, in mature age, and in the decline of life.

In *infancy* diseases of the brain and nervous system, notably, *convulsions*, rank first among the causes of death, *diseases of the lungs* have the second place, and *diarrhœal diseases* the third.

From the end of the first year of life to the end of the

fifth—that is to say in *early childhood*—the *infectious dis-eases*, especially scarlet fever and whooping-cough, give rise to the greatest mortality; then, as in infancy, next in order of mortality, at this period of life, come *lung diseases*, and third, the *diarrhœal diseases*.

In *childhood and early youth* (five to fifteen years) the *infectious diseases* are the chief causes of mortality, principally scarlet fever and continued fevers.

From *youth to manhood* (fifteen to twenty-five years) *phthisis* is the most important cause of death, and the infectious diseases sink to the second place.

In *early manhood* (twenty-five to thirty-five years) *phthisis* still maintains the first rank among the causes of death, but a marked increase in mortality is now observed from other diseases of the lungs. The infectious diseases continue to hold the second rank among the causes of death at this period of life.

In *manhood and maturity* (thirty-five to fifty-five years) *phthisis* maintains its predominance among the causes of death, but now the mortality from other diseases of the lungs becomes largely augmented. The second place in the order of causes of death at this period of life is taken by diseases of local origin, especially local affections of the brain and nervous system, of the heart and blood-vessels, and of the digestive organs; *cancer* now becomes an important source of mortality; but the infectious diseases sink to a comparatively low place among the causes of death.

In the *decline of life* (fifty-five to seventy-five years), the *diseases of local origin*, including diseases of the lungs, are the chief causes of death, phthisis, the infectious diseases and general diseases, as a rule, except cancer, becoming relatively less predominant. At this period of life, indeed, the causes of death foreshadow the more general decay of old age (seventy-five and upwards), where death, if it does not arise from the natural inability of the several organs, in the progress of decay, to continue their functions, unaffected by exterior circumstances, is mainly brought about by local accidents of the brain and nervous system, the heart and blood-vessels, irredeemably damaged in the course of the decay.

The progress of fatal disease through the several periods of life has, in fact, characteristic relations with the natural condition of the body at the different periods. The fatal diseases of infancy are significant of the immaturity and mobility of the infants' organs and functions. The fatal diseases of childhood relate, not so much to states of the system then in fullest vigour of vital reaction (to inherent conditions of the body, so to speak), and to the influence of the media in which we live, as to the accidental liability of exposure to morbific agencies current among populations, such as the contagions of the catching diseases, as, for example, scarlet-fever, small-pox, measles, typhus, &c. With the completion of manhood, diseases indicative of local degenerations of tissue begin to be predominant, and with each successive stage of life this predominance becomes more marked. In old age the degenerative changes, which at earlier periods of life are regarded as the signs of disease, now appear as the natural consequences of decay, and death becomes a physiological, not a pathological fact—as the termination of a natural life, not as the premature close of a life cut short by disease.

CHAPTER III.

THE CONDITIONS UNDER WHICH THE CAUSES OF PREMATURE DEATH OPERATE.

We now come to the consideration of *the conditions under which the causes of premature death operate.*

And, first, let it be observed that these causes operate with very different degrees of intensity in different parts of the kingdom. Thus while in their totality they kill the population inhabiting the agricultural districts south of London at a rate of about 1,500 annually in every 100,000 living, they kill the population of certain manufacturing

and mining districts at rates of about 2,200 (Merthyr
Tydvil), 2,500 (Newcastle-on-Tyne), 2,700 (Leeds), and
3,400 (Liverpool). The wide range of intensity of operation of these causes in different localities when regarded
as a whole is, as might be inferred and will presently be
shown, even more markedly observed in regard to the
distribution in various localities of the particular diseases
or class of diseases which contribute most to swell the
number of premature deaths. The study of the circumstances under which the difference of prevalence of these
diseases in different districts occurs, furnishes the clue
to the conditions under which the causes of premature
death operate.

And here it may be well, before entering upon an exa-
mination of the conditions of prevalence of the several
classes of disease which have been set forth as causes of
premature death, to interpose a caution as to districts in
which the rate of premature mortality is least. It has
become customary to speak of these districts as *healthy
districts*, and the Registrar-General has adopted (if, indeed,
he did not first use) this term with regard to them. The
phrase is eminently misleading and, indeed, mischievous.
The term *healthy* as applied to these districts is in reality
used relatively with regard to the greater mortality of
other districts. It will scarcely be maintained that people
live too long in these so-called *healthy* districts, or that

2

people die in them from unavoidable causes alone. The sources of their smaller mortality are generally sufficiently obvious, but they do not as a rule include the removal of such causes of premature death as man himself creates, and, indeed, are quite independent of any intelligent co-operation on his part. Conditions of unwholesomeness are relatively as rife among rural communities as in towns, and to describe the state of these communities with reference to their mortality as *healthy* is to state not only what is inaccurate but to justify the inaction of their sanitary authorities. What work of theirs, they ask, could make a healthy district more healthy? These districts of small mortality are the *least unhealthy* districts in the kingdom as compared with districts of great mortality—the large town districts, for example. But as a rule they are positively *unhealthy* as regards their capacity for wholesomeness. We have before us, while writing, a series of recent official reports issued by the Local Government Board referring to fatal prevalences of enteric fever, diphtheria, scarlet-fever, and diarrhœa in the so-called *healthy* districts of the Registrar General. It is necessary to have in mind, then, that the term *healthy district*, as things go in England at present, should read *least unhealthy district*.

Taking now the causes of premature death in the order

of their predominance, *diseases of the lungs*, including *phthisis*, first come under consideration.

It may perhaps be said that the predominance of diseases of the lungs among the causes of premature death is the penalty which England pays for her commercial pre-eminence.

Far from an insignificant amount of the mortality of infants and young children is caused by these diseases (346,705 deaths being occasioned by them under 5 years of age, during the ten years 1861–70, out of a total of 1,249,026 at all ages). But their fatality chiefly falls upon youths and adults (fifteen years to fifty-five years), and especially upon adults in the prime of life (twenty to thirty years). The rates of mortality from lung-disease range in various parts of the kingdom from a little over 1,000 per 100,000 living in some districts (the districts south of London, for example) to over 2,000 in others, and even to close upon 3,000 (Wolverhampton). Now the districts of excessive mortality from lung-diseases are the centres of certain special industries ; and a study of the circumstances under which these industries are pursued speedily discloses the conditions under which this cause of premature mortality operates in the several districts.

The common condition determining diseases of the lungs is the sudden alternations of temperature to which

persons are liable from exposure to weather. But this
condition it may be taken will act pretty equably upon
persons and communities in different parts of the
kingdom, varying chiefly with peculiarities of local topo-
graphy and individual proclivities, the latter an indeter-
minate quantity. But there are numerous artificially
created conditions which predispose to the operation of
the common determining condition—the sudden alternations of temperature—and it is upon the extent to which
these artificial conditions exist that the greater or less
prevalence of fatal lung-disease depends. We observe
these in their simplest state in our ordinary household
arrangements, where, in our eagerness to protect ourselves from cold or variable weather, we commonly box
ourselves up in atmospheres more or less fouled by domestic operations, by our own breathing and by the
insensible emanations from the body, by artificial lights
particularly, and by all the various sources of impurity
which needs the continuous and never-ceasing exercise
of the housewife's care, if any reasonable state of cleanliness of air and surroundings is to be obtained and
maintained. The lungs supplied with an impoverished
and vitiated air gradually lose that aptitude of resistance
to those alternations of temperature which occur in the
ordinary progress of weather and season, and the time
comes when a sudden change, aforetime unheeded and

harmless, checks the natural action of the breathing apparatus, and brings about the states known as inflammation of the air-tubes; *bronchitis*, or of the substance of the lung, *pneumonia*, or leads to change of the lung-tissue, perhaps unrecognised at first, but which may become one of the formidable diseases of youth and adult life, *consumption*. It must be obvious how, under the circumstances of nursery life as commonly carried out in this country, the infant and young child are peculiarly exposed to harm, even in the best houses and among the well-to-do classes, from the artificially created atmosphere in which they too generally live. And when we contemplate the conditions of life under which infants and young children exist among the poorest and least provident classes, especially in our large towns, where they are housed in atmospheres fetid with every odious product of human filth, and where in inclement weather warmth is mainly obtained from the huddling together of the living, we can understand how the delicate and sensitive breathing apparatus of infancy and childhood readily breaks down under the incessant irrigation of the filthy air which is breathed.

What may thus be observed in too many cases in our ordinary household life is observed also substantially in all the indoor occupations of youth and manhood. Each of these occupations has to be followed under artificial conditions of atmosphere all favourable to, and some directly active in, the production of lung-diseases.

The industries which contribute most to excessive prevalence of lung-diseases in particular localities are mining, metal-work and cutlery, pottery, flax-working, cotton and wool manufacture, straw-plaiting, glove-making, lace-making, and silk-working. In these several industries we have persons working in artificially created atmospheres, more or less fouled with their own breathing, or with the effluvia of putrefying filth, or, at certain periods, with the products of imperfect combustion of gas or other illuminating agent, or with the dust and dirt of their industry, or surcharged with moisture and highly heated.

These several sources of lung-disease are observed in greatest intensity under the conditions in which the miner works. Deep beneath the ground, in galleries which at the best admit of but an imperfect change of air, in an atmosphere impoverished of oxygen and apt to be fouled by a fuming lamp or by the escape of gas from the seams which are being opened, or by the smoke of gunpowder from blasting, and which is laden by the fine dust struck from the work, the miner pursues his arduous labours in circumstances fatal to the long-continued healthy play of the lungs. In coal-mines the dust from the coal is a source of mechanical irritation to the lung not unfrequently directly provocative of mischief; while the sudden ascent from the relatively hot and moist levels to the outer air is liable, in the colder season, to throw upon the imperfectly acting and exhausted lung work which it is quite incapable of rightly performing, and failure in performance of which means disease.

In metal-work, cutlery, and pottery, especially the grinding and polishing of cutlery and the scouring of pottery, the adamantine dust from the processes named, which pervades the air of the workshops, becomes a special source of lung-disease. The irritative effect of steel-dust upon the grinder's lungs, and its influence in producing the very fatal form of disease known as *grinder's-consumption*, is one of the most painful studies in the whole range of industrial diseases.

In the cotton manufacture the work is largely carried on in rooms highly heated, and containing an undue amount of moisture in the atmosphere, with much fine dust. The same is true also, to some extent, in the woollen manufacture. The transition from these rooms, after several hours' confinement in them, to the outer atmosphere when the temperature is low, and with rarely any sufficient amount of additional clothing to protect the worker from the cold, is undoubtedly provocative of lung-disease.

Finally, in straw-plaiting, glove-making, and lace-making, when carried out in the workers' rooms, we observe the causes which are apt to foster lung-diseases in our houses operating in great intensity. Carried on, for the most part, in small, ill-ventilated, often damp, and otherwise ill-found cottages, which are cold in winter and unbearably hot in summer, in an atmosphere usually pervaded with filthy emanations coming largely from the outside, the work is pursued by women, many of them hardly out of girlhood, and by not a few children. Under such conditions they work for many hours, sometimes twelve or fourteen, of the day; producing there a close resemblance, in the deficient ventilation, the sedentary occupation, the want of active bodily exercise, and a listless state of mind, a state of things approximating to what aforetime had been found to exist and to prove so productive of lung-disease in gaols.

Although the circumstances under which the above-named industries are pursued favours the development of all lung-diseases, including phthisis, there are certain important differences in the conditions which affect the production of phthisis as compared with other diseases which it is necessary to note.

Phthisis is especially the lung-disease of youth and early manhood; other lung-diseases predominate in infancy and early childhood, and in the latter half of life.

This predominance of phthisis during the more actively occupied working ages is itself significant of the influence of industrial occupations upon its prevalence, and its occurrence is notably allied to sedentary labours pursued in ill-ventilated rooms, amidst fouled atmospheres. But it has been recently ascertained that there is a widely operating condition which exercises a most important influence in predisposing persons to the degenerative changes in the lungs which we call phthisis. This condition is *dampness of soil.* Eminent authorities in England and America have shown, each independently of the other, that *dampness of soil is an important cause of phthisis to the population living upon it.* It is difficult to exaggerate the practical value of this conclusion in relation to sanitary work and administration.

Infectious Diseases, such as scarlet-fever, the continued fevers (typhus, enteric fever, &c.), measles, diphtheria, small-pox, malignant cholera, &c., hold the second place in order of magnitude among the causes of premature death. The number of deaths from these diseases during the ten years 1861–70 exceeded 700,000 (of these deaths about 576,000 occurred in infancy and early childhood, up to five years). The distribution of these deaths in different parts of the kingdom manifests much greater

variations than have been observed in the case of lung-
diseases, and the differences in the prevalence are as sug-
gestive as in the last-named class of diseases of the conditions under which dangerous infectious diseases operate.
It is necessary, for a clear apprehension of this part of
our subject, to deal separately with each of the more
important diseases which enter into the class of infectious
diseases. But before doing this, it will be well to explain
in what sense the word infectious is used here, and also
to note an important distinction which separates the
several sorts of diseases into two classes.

Much confusion has arisen, and still arises, in the use
of the terms *contagion* and *infection*. There was a time
when each word was used in a particular sense, and the
transmission of a disease by contact (contagion), and of a
disease by pollution of the air with the transmitting
material (infection) were believed to represent cardinal
differences in the propagation of the transmissible diseases.
It is now known that the distinction originally implied in
the terms does not exist, that there is no such thing as
mere *contact* transmission of the diseases in question, and
that the phenomenon of transmission is by no means
confined to diffusion of the transmissible material in the
air. Hence both the words *contagion* and *infection* are
now used technically and generally as convertible terms,
typifying, as applied to disease, the property of its trans-

missibility in some way or other from the sick to the healthy. It would have been well if both words could have been discarded, for a tradition of their former use still attaches to them, but they would seem to have become permanently fixed in the language. The tradition of old use adheres, however, more firmly to the word *contagion* than to the word *infection;* and even at the present day we find persons bewildering themselves and confusing others by using the former word in a sense which has long ago ceased to be in force, and which, in fact, is meaningless in the present state of medical science. We have here adopted the word *infection* and its derivatives in preference to the word *contagion* and its derivatives, as the former is less apt to trip up the reader by the false lights of old associations than the latter.

There is a general question relating to *infection* which may, perhaps, be as well referred to here as elsewhere in this primer. Persons exist who believe that the *infection* of the various infectious diseases operates quite independently of the conditions which govern the development and prevalence of most other diseases. Given the *infection*, the phenomenon of its spread follows, according to these persons, as a matter of course. Now, all the *infections* are influenced in their spread and prevalence, although in different degrees, by certain well-understood conditions, some peculiar to the individual, some peculiar to his surroundings, some peculiar to the locality in which he is placed, some peculiar to seasons of the year; and it should be clearly understood that our ability to limit the prevalence of *infections* is dependent upon our knowledge of these conditions, and of our capability to remove them.

The infectious diseases admit of being divided into two classes with reference to the circumstances under which they exist. This division involves a distinction that has an important practical bearing, as will be seen in the sequel.

Several of these diseases, as for example small-pox, scarlet-fever, and measles, have originated in remote ages under conditions of life of which we can form no conception in the present day. We know nothing of the causation of these diseases, except as coming to us by successive transmission from period to period, from country to country, from nation to nation, from person to person. They are never absent from among us, at one time existing only in a few scattered centres, at another spreading over the whole people as an *epidemic*. The infectious diseases, indeed, are especially designated epidemic diseases from this notable phenomenon of general prevalence at intervals. *Epidemic* is a word which in its proper signification is descriptive, and simply means general prevalence in a community, or a district, or a country. Certain mysterious technical meanings have been attached to the word which are nothing more than concealments of an ignorance which even the learned need not be ashamed to admit. The word *epidemic*, when used of disease, or of any other phenomenon to which it is applicable, should be used simply in its ordinary and proper sense, as defined by Webster, to wit: " Common to, or affecting, a whole people, or a great number in a community ; prevalent; general."

Others of the infectious diseases, as the continued fevers (typhus, enteric fever, relapsing fever), diphtheria, influenza, and malignant cholera, probably have their origin in conditions which recur at intervals, or which habitually exist among us, or which are produced in certain social convulsions. Thus influenza would appear to depend .for its origin, as well as for its prevalence, upon as yet undetermined meteorological conditions ; diphtheria is so closely allied with sundry sources of domestic insalubrity which apparently affect houses in the country more markedly than in the town, that it would appear to have its origin in a particular com-bination of these as yet unknown ; enteric fever seems to be born out of the excremental filth amongst which large sections of our population live ; typhus and relaps-ing fever are the products of overcrowding, privation, and

absolute famine, as different degrees of this trinity of foul-
ness, want, and suffering obtain ; while malignant cholera,
known to us only in England as a terrible importation
at intervals from our great dependency in the East, is
believed to be a product of excremental filth, acted
upon by a tropical sun, under the conditions mainly
found among the low-lying lands in the delta of the
Ganges.

The infectious diseases which have had origin at a
remote period, under conditions which have probably
disappeared, and the infectious diseases which may
originate under conditions existing at the present time,
present themselves in their practical aspect in different
lights, as we shall see presently.

Before entering upon the consideration of the several
principal infectious diseases existing in this country, we
may note in passing a remarkable phenomenon under
observation at the present time. The one infectious
disease which has become historical, and which, from
the ravages it committed in the middle ages, has been
written indelibly on the pages of history, *plague*, after
the extensive outbreak which was marked in this country
by what is known as the "Great Plague of London"
(1665), gradually died out in Europe and the Levant, and
eventually disappeared. This disease has shown itself

anew in various places, and at various times, within the last twenty years in some of its former haunts in the Levant, and during the. last five years it has given indications of once more becoming a formidable pestilence. It has arisen afresh under long-continued states of indescribable filth and misery, and in its development and course follows closely the habits of typhus.

To proceed now to a consideration of the several more fatal infectious diseases, and the conditions under which they prevail.

Scarlet-fever is the most fatal to life of the infectious diseases common to this country. During the ten years 1861-70, it caused no less than 207,867 deaths, of which 133,462—nearly nine-tenths—occurred among infants and children under five years of age, and 188,557 by the time of expiry of the ninth year. In fact, scarlet-fever kills yearly, on the average, about 21,000 persons, chiefly children not exceeding ten years of age. This disease has been called the "English Pestilence." The distribution of the mortality caused by it over the kingdom is marked by great irregularity. There are localities in which for a period of years no deaths occur from scarlet-fever, and from which it is known that the disease has been wholly absent. On the other hand there are localities where the disease, always being present, deaths from it form one of the most regular features of the mortality returns. The rate of mortality from scarlet-fever per 100,000 living at the ages referred to, during the ten years 1861-70, ranged from 12 at all ages, and 119 at ages under five years (Builth, Brecknock), to 186 and 760 at the same ages respectively (Gateshead), and 215 and 854 (Easington).

The chief districts of constant excessive mortality from scarlet-fever are London, the Tyne-side towns, and the mining districts of Durham, Northumberland, some parts of Cumberland (Carlisle, Cockermouth, White-haven), the manufacturing districts of Lancashire, Cheshire, and the West Riding, Birmingham, Wolver-hampton and the vicinity, the potteries of Staffordshire, Bristol, and Flint county. These localities constitute the *scarlet-fever fields* of the kingdom. There the disease is continuously cultivated, and from thence it presumably spreads at intervals, sweeping over the entire kingdom. In the greater number of these places it is known that there are great agglomerations of populations of young children, but these agglomerations are not peculiar to these localities alone. The special conditions which determine the fatal prevalence of scarlet-fever in the localities named have not yet been made, strange to say, a subject of detailed investigation, although such investigation gives the greatest promise of our being able to provide for the arrest of a starting epidemic of scarlet-fever at the source.

The *Continued Fevers—typhus, relapsing fever, enteric fever*—stand next in order of fatality to scarlet-fever among the infectious diseases. They caused 189,285 deaths during the ten years 1861–70, of which a seventh only (26,630) occurred under ten years of age.

Typhus is pre-eminently the fever of overcrowding and destitution—of an overcrowding and destitution which happily are becoming things of the past in this country. Wherever overcrowding and destitution are pushed to the extreme, and where these conditions concur with, or follow. close upon, great fatigue, there typhus almost invariably makes its appearance. We have thus seen it developed among the Turkish forces and some portions of the Russian forces in the war just ended, and the disease is at the present moment spreading broad-cast in the districts and among the soldiers at the seats of war in Eastern Europe and Armenia. This event was looked for as inevitable when the Turkish commissariat arrangements failed, and when the half-starved men, exhausted with fatigue, clad miserably in rags, were compelled to seek warmth by close-packing in their tents and in the houses of the peasantry, under indescribable conditions of filth. The conditions which gave rise to the disease

3

were the conditions which favoured most its spread by
infection. Once developed, the disease has spared none
coming within its infective influence; and the civil populations of the districts occupied by the opposing armies, and
to which the sick, the wounded, and prisoners have been
sent, are now contributing to a mortality which, in the
end, will probably prove larger than the mortality caused
by sickness and wounds among the troops during the
campaign.

There are states of destitution which would seem
to give rise to the infection of typhus, the infecting
persons themselves not suffering from the disease. In
1868, when famine prevailed in Algeria, the starving
Arabs flocked into the towns in the utmost state of misery
and privation. It was observed that many of these
miserables, as they craved relief or lay about in corners,
or beneath such cover as afforded some sort of shelter,
exhaled a penetrative putrefactive odour in their breath
and from their bodies—in other words, that, still living,
they were apparently putrefying. No symptoms of fever
or other acute disease were observed, but the persons who
came in contact with them were rapidly struck down
with typhus, which, thus lighted up, spread on all sides.

Typhus, as ordinarily observed, is peculiarly a disease
of towns.

Relapsing fever appears in much the same conditions

as give rise to typhus, but it has more marked relations with famine, and hence is popularly known as *famine-fever*.

Enteric fever is a special product of putrefying human excrement, under conditions not yet fully known. Originating in excrement, the excremental matters of the sick who suffer from it possess the power of producing the disease in others, not less definitely than the breath and emanations from a case of small-pox or of scarlet-fever or of measles, will produce small-pox or scarlet-fever or measles, as the case may be. Enteric fever is so universally distributed in the kingdom, and the mode of production by the infective discharges of the sick from the disease has become so much the more common mode, that it is difficult in any given case to exclude the probability of infection. Be this as it may, the occurrence of enteric fever means that the sufferer has taken into his system, by breathing or swallowing, a sufficiency of putrefying excrement, or of excrement to which special infective qualities have been given by having passed through the bowels of a person affected with enteric fever, or of the special morbid products of the two sorts of excrement. He has swallowed or breathed, as the case may be, the actual stuff or its products, as presented to him in the form of an emanation coming from the filthy open privy pits which still disgrace a large portion of the land, or as a cloud of dust wafted into public places where the stuff has been promiscuously scattered on the surface of the earth, or as it has been conveyed to him suspended in the air which has intruded upon his privacy or permeated his residence from an improperly arranged cesspool or ill-ordered drain, or as he has drunk it unsuspectingly in water or as distributed in milk. Enteric fever, indeed, is the household and municipal fever of this kingdom. Its prevalence and persistence is the surest indication of the failure of householders and local authorities in having secured, the former their families, the latter the communities under their charge, from the mischievous action of the most repulsive filth.

Malignant Cholera.—This formidable infective disease appears in England only at intervals. It takes its origin in India, principally in the low-lying lands of the Lower Provinces of Bengal, especially within the delta of the Ganges. There the disease does not appear to be ever absent, and occasionally it breaks out with great intensity, manifesting at the same time an extraordinary diffusiveness. While usually this diffusiveness is limited to India, and the conditions on which it commonly depends do not exist beyond the coast line or the northern boundary of that country, when the exceptional diffusiveness referred to declares itself, the malady is no longer restricted in its development and power of propagation within the limits of the Indian peninsula. At such times, wherever persons sick of the disease carry it, there it exhibits similar phenomena to those observed in its Indian home, takes temporary root, and grows in any locality favourable for its reproduction into which it may be imported. Each place where it is thus planted becomes a new centre of propagation, and so by successive infections of localities it may traverse the whole world.

Now the local conditions which favour the development of cholera are similar to those which favour the development of enteric fever ; and there is good reason for the belief that the infective quality of cholera, as of enteric fever, rests in the intestinal discharges of the patient. The conditions under which cholera spreads in this country are thus stated in the official memorandum issued by the Local Government Board, for the information of sanitary authorities—a memorandum prepared for that Board by its former Medical Officer, the great master in sanitary science and craft in this country, John Simon :—
" It is characteristic of cholera, not only of the disease in its developed and alarming form, but equally of the slightest diarrhœa which the epidemic influence can cause, that all matters which the patient discharges from his stomach and bowels are infective, and that, if they be left without disinfection after they are discharged, their infectiveness during some days gradually grows stronger and stronger.

Probably, under ordinary circumstances, the patient has
no power of infecting other persons except by means of
these discharges, nor any power of infecting even by
them, except in so far as particles of them are enabled to
taint the food, water, or air which people consume. Thus,
when a case of cholera is imported into any place, the
disease is not likely to spread, unless in proportion as it
finds locally open to it certain facilities for spreading by
indirect infection. In order rightly to appreciate what
these facilities must be, the following considerations have
to be borne in mind :—*first*, that any choleraic discharge
cast without previous thorough disinfection into any cesspool or drain, or other depository or conduit of filth,
infects the excremental matters with which it there
mingles, and probably to some extent, the effluvia which
those matters evolve ; *secondly*, that the infective power of
choleraic discharges attaches to whatever bedding, clothing,
towels, and like things have been imbued with them, and
renders these things, if not thoroughly disinfected, as
capable of spreading the disease in places to which they
are sent (for washing or other purposes) as, in like circumstances, the cholera patient himself would be ; *thirdly*,
that if, by leakage or soakage from cesspools or drains, or
through reckless casting out of slops and wash-water, any
taint (however small) of the infective material gets access
to wells or other sources of drinking-water, it imparts to

enormous volumes of water the power of propagating the disease. When due regard is had to these possibilities of indirect infection, there will be no difficulty in understanding that even a single case of cholera, perhaps of the slightest degree, and perhaps quite unsuspected in a neighbourhood, may, *if local circumstances co-operate*, exert a terribly infective power on considerable masses of population."

Malignant cholera has prevailed epidemically in England four times, namely, in 1831-32, in 1848-49, in 1854, and in 1866. The following is a table of the mortality occasioned by the disease in the several visits, exclusive of diarrhœa :—

	Deaths from Cholera.
1831-32	30,924
1848-49	54,398
1854	20,097
1865-66	14,378
	119,797

Whooping-cough (as also *influenza*) has still to be numbered among the diseases of which the conditions of prevalence, otherwise than as they are spread by infection, are unknown. Whooping-cough caused, during the ten years 1861-70, 112,800 deaths.

Measles caused 94,099 deaths during the ten years 1861-70, and its mortality ranged within this period from

126 per 100,000 living, in the least unhealthy districts, to 608 (Warrington), 610 (Abergavenny), 624 (Wigan), and 722 (Liverpool). We know nothing of the history of measles except as a transmitted infection from the sick to the well. Of all the permanent infections measles is the most difficult to deal with preventively, as the disease becomes infectious during the three or four days' indisposition which precedes the eruption, and when, very commonly, the child still associates with its companions, and its indisposition is not heeded. Measles varies very greatly in its intensity in different epidemics; sometimes prevailing as a most malignant malady, sometimes, and more frequently, as one of the slightest of specific ailments.

Diphtheria, within the period last named (1861–70), had occasioned 39,454 deaths. The history of this fatal infectious disease goes back to remote times. Unlike that of small-pox and scarlet-fever, the history is not one of continuous propagation by infection. Difficult as it is to deny all chances of infection in a country where the malady is naturalised, yet the most careful observers appear to have come to the conclusion that the disease not unfrequently springs up anew among us. The conditions under which these apparently new growths are observed have been, in towns, markedly connected with exposure of the subjects of the disease to the air of imperfectly ventilated sewers and drains ; and in the rural districts, in addition, to the filthy surroundings of ill-kept farmsteads. The disease has a certain preference for country districts as compared with town districts ; and dampness of houses or of soil seems to play some part in its localisation.

Small-pox, although ranking last but one in the order of mortality caused by infectious diseases, caused not less than 34,786 deaths in the ten years 1861–70. Of all the infectious diseases this is perhaps the least affected in prevalence by individual and external conditions, setting aside the artificial condition of vaccination. There are exceptional persons who, irrespective of vaccination, resist the infectiousness of small-pox ; and the disease itself is apparently influenced in its activity by season. It is true that the time of its greatest activity in this country, the colder months of the year, is the time when persons, keeping more to their houses, the chances of dissemination among families are augmented ; but in India, where the influence of meteorological changes admit of being more clearly discriminated in respect to the disease, there seems to be no doubt that the potency of the small-pox infection, as that of vaccine virus, is diminished during the hot season. It is reasonable to infer, then, that some part of the fluctuation of small-pox in this country depends directly, and not indirectly,

upon seasonal influence. There are reasons for the
belief also that local conditions of population may affect
the degree of infectiveness of small-pox.

The great epidemic of 1871–72 was unexampled in the
memory of living man for the diffusiveness of the disease
and its malignancy. Now the starting-point of this
epidemic, it is averred by a very thoughtful and com-
petent observer, Léon Colin, was in a part of Brittany.
There, shortly before the siege of Paris, small-pox ap-
peared among a population unprotected by vaccination.
The disease declared itself with a malignancy only observed in the first instance among populations so placed,
and under ordinary circumstances it would probably
have exhausted itself in the district where it assumed
this character (so slight was the communication between
it and the surrounding country), or at the worst would
have extended in a scattered and manageable form into
the districts immediately adjacent. But the exigencies
of the Franco-German war brought about a state of things
which, according to our authority, converted what would
otherwise have been an exceptionally severe local outbreak of small-pox, which would have served alone to
point a local vaccination-moral, into a world-wide dissemination of a malignancy so great as to compel the
serious attention of Governments. First, it was necessary
to draft into the French army, to the utmost limit, con-

scripts and recruits from the infected district; secondly, it was found impossible to carry out in time of war those precautions as to vaccination and re-vaccination of persons added to the army which are insisted upon in time of peace. So it happened that the conscripts and recruits from the infected locality in Brittany carried with them into the army the malignant disease prevalent in their homes. The army at the time furnished an abundancy of unvaccinated and imperfectly vaccinated individuals for the reception and propagation of the disease in an unmodified state. As the army moved hither and thither it spread the disease among the civil population, and prisoners and wounded taken by the Germans carried the malady among the German forces and into Germany. Paris early received the infection from detachments of troops, having the disease among them, who marched into the city before the siege; and there, shut in, the malady multiplied under circumstances peculiarly favourable for retaining its malignancy. With the raising of the siege and the resumption of communication between Paris and the outer world, the first out-rush of the released inhabitants and foreigners who had had to remain within the city during the investment, scattered the malady broadcast in hitherto unaffected provinces, to adjacent countries which to that time had remained unaffected, and among other countries to England.

At the time of this importation London was beginning to suffer from one of the recurrent epidemics of small-pox, which mark the accumulation of unvaccinated people in or during the period of indifference which customarily follows the alarm of a present epidemic. But the character of the disease which marked the beginning of the epidemic was wholly different as to intensity from that which was imported from Paris when the siege was raised, and which, displaying an unusual infectiveness as well as malignancy, presently supplanted the existing disease, and gave that aspect to the subsequent progress of the epidemic in the metropolis, and afterwards in the country, which marked it. This fact had been ascertained at the time, and long before the origin above assigned to the great outbreak had been ascertained and made known. The history of the epidemic in London and in England generally is consistent with the account we have given; and the history of the progress of the epidemic in other countries, extending over a great portion of the surface of the globe, is also consistent with it.

The origin assigned to this small-pox epidemic suggests a line of observation and practice respecting other infectious diseases of considerable moment. It is not impossible that the occasionally observed malignancy of other infectious diseases, especially scarlet-fever, measles, and diphtheria, may in the first instance be the result of local conditions especially favouring such a development of the malady. It is now known that the virulence of an infective product of disease may be cultivated to an extraordinary pitch in the laboratory. A phenomenon that can be artificially produced may also, it is to be presumed, be naturally produced, and the excessive virulence sometimes observed in the action of the small-pox, the scarlet-fever, the measles, and the diphtheria infections may at times undergo a course of undesigned cultivation under peculiar local and individual circumstances similar to that which has been observed of other sorts of virulent morbid products in the laboratory. This is a possibility which it is now necessary to keep well in mind, in view of the phenomena of malignancy showing themselves in connection with any of the ordinary infectious diseases; because, even pending the determination of the scientific question, such malignancy should influence the precautionary measures adopted to prevent the spread of the disease, by giving to them the greatest stringency of which they are practicable.

Popular observation has long anticipated what will presently become probably an important scientific truth, namely, that a severe form of infectious disease, in transmission, begets a severe form. Medical science has hitherto dwelt upon the reverse of this belief, namely, that a mild form of infectious disease in one person may

beget the severest form in another ; but it has not fully
pursued the relations of the more malignant disease as
to degree of virulence in successive transmissions. Now
it is not uncommon to hear mothers, who look to the
occurrence of scarlet-fever and measles among their
young children as an ordinary and unavoidable incident
of child-life which it is desirable to get over as early as
practicable, express the wish, when a mild type of scarlet-
fever or measles is prevalent, that their children would,
on account of this mildness, " catch " the disease then.

Diseases of the brain and nervous system, including
hydrocephalus, hold the third place in rank among the
causes of premature death.   This position is almost
wholly due to the preponderance of "convulsions" as
a cause of death in infancy among the diseases of this
class.   During the ten years 1861–70, 669,899 deaths
were caused by maladies of this sort, of which numbers
249,990 occurred in infancy, and 106,883 between infancy
and the completion of the fourth year of life.   These
diseases fall to their lowest point as causes of death in
adult life, to increase again as life advances and old age
steals on.

The fatal diseases of the nervous system which occur
in the decline of and in advanced life may be taken in
the main to be the results of degenerative changes going
on in the nervous tissues, which are, in fact, for the most

part, the changes of natural and often premature decay. On the other hand, the fatal diseases of the. nervous system in infancy and early childhood are, in a large proportion of cases, the indications of an immaturity or defective vitality or original vice of organisation related to the class of developmental diseases so called, which we shall have next to refer to. At the best, the mobile and impressible nervous system of the infant responds to exterior influences and impressions in a manner very different from that commonly observed later in life. Morbid conditions, which, in late childhood, in youth, and in manhood, are manifested by shiverings, appear in the infant to be manifested by convulsions. But the question that most concerns us here is that the prevalences of diseases manifested by brain symptoms in infancy and early childhood, especially the prevalence of convulsions, is obviously influenced by certain local insanitary conditions. The rate of mortality from diseases of the nervous system, including hydrocephalus, ranges in England from 675 per 100,000 living under five years of age in the least unhealthy districts of the kingdom, to 1456 in the North-Western Counties, and 1504 in London.

The most striking instance of the influence of local insanitary conditions upon excessive local prevalences of these diseases is obtained from what is known of the effects of a vitiated state of the atmosphere in promoting convulsions.　About the beginning of the century very many of the children born in the Dublin lying-in hospital died of what were termed "nine-day fits," in other words, fatal convulsions, which ordinarily set in about the ninth day after birth.　The master of the hospital, at that time Dr. Clarke, came to the conclusion that much of this excessive mortality from convulsions among the infants depended upon the foul state of the atmosphere, which existed in the then very imperfectly ventilated wards.　Acting upon this opinion, measures were adopted for improving the ventilation, a marked diminution in the numbers of fatal cases of "nine-day fits" following. These measures were still further developed, the rate of mortality from the nine-day fits diminishing with each successive improvement.　In the end the mortality among the new-born children was reduced to a *sixty-eighth* part of what it had been when the first measures for a more effective ventilation of the wards had been adopted.

The latest contribution to our knowledge of the influence of a vitiated atmosphere in causing the convulsive disorders of childhood comes to us from Calcutta, where the mortality for infants is enormous from this cause. Surgeon-Major Arthur Payne, M.D., the Health Officer for that city, thus describes the conditions under which the children of the native population are born, and in which an attempt is made to rear them during the early days of infancy :—

" A chamber, a few feet square, so situated that at the best of times its atmosphere must be close, has every aperture carefully shut. It is crowded with relatives and attendants, so that there is barely room to sit, and a fire of wood embers, or even charcoal, is burning in an open vessel. The atmosphere is principally smoke, which is increased by herbs scattered on the fire for the purpose. The woman is lying generally on the ground in the midst of this. The feeling on entering the room is that of impending suffocation, and the first step which the visitor takes is to enable himself to breathe. He opens the window and clears the room of as many persons as can be got to leave it, who betake themselves to a balcony outside, or block the doorway until his departure. He knows full well that, as soon as his back is turned, all will be as it was when he arrived ; for it is among the first principles of native midwifery that air should be kept away from a newly born child. This process of asphyxiation seems to be carried on for a variable period, but in no case, as far as I can ascertain, is the period less than seven days.; it often extends to ten, and with Mahomedans much longer ; nor does it alter under any extremes of natural heat. No argument is needed to connect this state of things with a high

4

prevalence of infantile fever, but it is both necessary and interesting to trace its relation to the enormous quantity of fatal convulsive disease that occurs here during the first days of life; for not only is there a total of 4908 cases recorded under the two heads [convulsions and tetanus], but I find that no less than one-half of the entire number of deaths, viz. 8,005, took place within a fortnight. . . . . . If this be true in substantial native houses, nothing more need be said of the huts which the masses of the population inhabit, unless it be that the poorest people use cow-dung for fuel, while they have not, as the others have, the little ventilation which a cold outer air will enforce in spite of all endeavours to prevent it."

General diseases, so called, other than the infectious as commonly known, have the fourth place in order of predominance among the causes of premature death, and among these diseases the foremost position is held by *cancer,* the *wasting of infants* (mesenteric wasting), *croup, scrofula,* and *rheumatism.*

Cancer caused 82,820 deaths during the ten years 1861–70. This formidable malady is of the rarest until after the twenty-fifth year of age. Between the twenty-fifth and thirty-fifth year of age the mortality from it begins to increase; after the thirty-fifth year the augmentation is considerable; and the maximum is attained between the fifty-fifth and sixty-fifth year. The disease, in fact, is markedly a disease of adult life. As yet there is, unhappily, no clue to the causes of this dreadful malady, but recent advances in medical knowledge of the mode of development of the disease gives reasonable hope that, at some probably not far distant period, we shall obtain an insight as to the conditions which determine it. Cancer has a tendency to run in families; but the assumption that the inherited cancerous state affects the whole body does not therefore follow. Recent researches tend to show that cancer is primarily a local affection, and that the general state of indisposition which marks its progress is the result of a gradual infection of the system, through the blood, with the cancerous products of the local disease. It is difficult to believe that, if this view of cancer prove to be accurate, it will not lead to important consequences both in the medical, the surgical, and the preventive treatment of the malady.

The *mesenteric wasting of infants*, and *scrofula* (when the former name is not used, as is too often the case, to designate the wasting arising from rickets), belong to the same category of disease production in which phthisis and hydrocephalus are included. The same morbid cause, acting in different organs, produces the various results which have received the several names given, namely, in the lungs, phthisis; in the brain and its membranes, hydrocephalus; in certain of the abdominal glands, mesenteric wasting; and in the general glandular system, scrofula. The medical doctrine of the conditions under which these diseases are developed is becoming more hopeful in view of prevention, as in the case of cancer. In these tubercular diseases also it is now beginning to be understood that the starting-point, as in cancer, is a local affection, and that the general affection of the system, or the manifestation of other local centres of disease, is the result of a gradual infection through the blood with the tuberculous products of the centre first formed. Medicine is beginning to see its way to clearer conceptions of the conditions liable to determine the commencing local mischief, and these conceptions indicate possible future ways of controlling phthisis, and presumably the congenerous diseases.

Rheumatism has not only an important place among the premature causes of death, but it is one of the most important causes of disablement. It is especially a disease arising from cold and damp, whether as experienced in sudden alternations, or in continuous exposure. In this country the disease has peculiarly important relations with the conditions under which a large proportion of the rural population live. In the rural districts the disease is probably less a question of exposure to the weather than of housing. The foster-beds of rheumatism here—as also in town districts where like conditions of housing obtain —are the too numerous cottages, and even houses of a better class, which have been built without any provision to protect them from the damp of the soil, without sufficient means of lighting and ventilation, and of which even the walls are apt to retain moisture like a sponge. Such houses—damp and chilly, often not weather-proof, incapable of being properly warmed by the biggest fire or the hottest sun, and from which the outer air is as much as possible excluded in order to keep in the buildings such warmth as may be given to them—are the foster-beds of rheumatism. And when, as too commonly happens, they are occupied by families whose means are hardly separated from destitution, rheumatism becomes one of the most important agencies in producing degeneration of race.

The *developmental diseases* (exclusive of old age), namely, atrophy and debility, premature birth, teething, childbirth, &c., have the fifth place in the order of causes of premature death. These diseases derive their generic name of *developmental* from their being chiefly incident to particular periods of the growth of the frame. Thus *teething* includes the deaths of infants and young children which happen during the development of the first set of teeth—the milk-teeth—and for which no other cause appears to be assignable than the disturbance of the system, which at times accompanies this development. *Atrophy* and *debility* include, for the most part, deaths of infants who from birth, owing to defective conditions of· the digestive organs, appear to be incapable of appropriating the nourishment given to them, and waste away, or who appear to die from imperfect vitality, or who are the victims of bad management. *Premature birth* includes the deaths of children who have been born at a time when they were so undeveloped as to be incapable of sustaining life after birth. *Childbirth* includes the deaths incident to the parturient state.

But in so far as the developmental diseases affect infancy, they are in great part indications of degenerative changes of race. They are chiefly observed under conditions in which communities have been exposed, generation after generation, to states of occupation and of living which have brought about marked degradation of type in the individuals composing it. Thus they are notably observed in those mining and manufacturing districts, and in those towns and country districts where numbers of people live who, in the best of times, earn only a bare subsistence; who earn that subsistence by prolonged labour underground, or in unwholesome workshops, and who have in their homes to herd together under conditions of filth and over-crowding which are shocking even when contemplated in the herding of brute beasts. Under circumstances such as these, great numbers of our industrial population have in course of time become stunted in body and mind, and subject to degenerative changes affecting the different parts of the system, each change marking a degradation of vitality, and not a few of these changes capable of being transmitted, together with the deteriorated frame, from parents to children.

This description refers only to one phase of degeneration of race, as it is observed in a civilised country such as England; but this phase is immeasurably the most important with reference to the public health. Degenerations of race are by no means confined to the industrial classes. Each order of life presents some form or other of them, but among the orders who live under conditions of well-being these degenerations are observed mainly as the result of pernicious habits, such as the excessive use of intoxicating liquors (not peculiar to these orders, but among them the evil influence of such excess as a degenerative agency may be more clearly distinguished and closely observed), and of certain maladies, such as the tubercular (consumption being an example), and the cancerous, of which the tendency to may be transmitted in families.

One of the most formidable consequences of these

degenerations of race is observed in the great proportion
of immature children born among the people subject to
them, and of children actually diseased at the time of birth.
The terms "premature birth," "teething," "atrophy and
debility," among the developmental diseases; " convulsions " and " hydrocephalus," among diseases of the brain
and nervous system; and the "wasting of infants" and
" scrofula" among the general diseases, largely cover
conditions of the system, tubercular or other, which are
expressions of a state of degeneration.   And when this
degeneration has not been such as to destroy life in
infancy, its results are observed in after-life, influencing
or determining the incidence of numerous forms of
disabling or fatal disease, while the degeneration may
be propagated from parents to children through several
generations.

And again, the terms above-named include also very many
deaths of infants who succumb to inanition from insufficient or improper feeding, or to the form of mal-nutrition
known as *rickets*.   Rickets has scarcely a place among
the causes of death enumerated in the Registrar-General's
returns, yet it is one of the commonest sources of the
fatal "wasting," the " convulsions," and the " bronchitis"
of infants and young children.   In fact, inanition, or, in
other words, starvation, simple or in a modified form,
such as results in rickets, too frequently concurs with and

aggravates those degenerative changes which have been inherited by the infant ; and, independently of such changes, it has a most important place among the conditions promoting the large waste of life among infants and young children.

Diseases of the Heart occupy the sixth place in the order of the causes of premature death. These diseases are, with few exceptions, the results of pre-existing morbid conditions, which would fall within other categories. Thus they are determined by scarlet-fever, by rheumatism, by gout, by syphilis, by degenerative disease of the kidney, tubercular disease, &c. Heart-disease is also one of the morbid conditions brought about by excessive indulgence in alcoholic drinks. Finally, the heart-disease of mid-life and advancing years is not unfrequently the result of the degeneration of tissues, prematurely manifested, which characterises the normal degeneration of old age. It is not until after the twenty-fifth year of life that heart-disease begins to assume a prominent position as a cause of premature death, and it becomes more and more prominent in each succeeding decade until the age of seventy-five years. Very much of the fatal heart-disease of manhood and mid-life has been the slowly developed consequence of mischief in the organ determined by scarlet-fever in childhood, and rheumatic fever during adolescence.

Heart-disease was credited with 288,447 deaths during the ten years 1861-70, that is to say, 6 per cent. of the total mortality from all causes.

Diseases of the Digestive Organs come seventh in order as causes of premature death. Of these diseases those characterised by looseness of the bowels, the diarrhœal diseases, to wit, diarrhœa, home-bred cholera, and flux (dysentery) stand pre-eminent. The cholera, to which reference has been made before in the section on infectious diseases—malignant cholera—must not be confounded with the common cholera of this climate. We know malignant cholera in this country only as an imported disease; but the home-bred cholera, although resembling the malignant in some of its symptoms, has a wholly different history in its development. Much confusion has been caused and exists from one and the same name being commonly applied to both diseases, namely, "cholera," and it would seem as if this source of confusion could not be eradicated. At least this is the conclusion which seems inevitable from the Royal College of Physicians having retained the same name for both diseases, and sought to distinguish the one from the other by the affix of the designation "simple" to the home-bred cholera and "malignant" to the cholera of foreign origin. It is true that the diarrhœal diseases noted in this section, namely, simple cholera, diarrhœa, and dysentery, are governed in their prevalence by the like local conditions which govern the prevalence of malignant cholera, and also of enteric fever, namely, conditions of excremental pollution of air, of soil, or of water. But in the case of the home-bred cholera, ordinary diarrhœa, and bowel flux, these seem to be determined as to prevalence by the products of the common putrefaction of excremental filth at certain seasons of the year, especially in the later summer and autumn, and particularly by high ranges of temperature at these seasons. On the other hand, while malignant cholera and enteric fever equally have close relations as to prevalence with the existence of putrefying excremental filth *something else* than the ordinary products of putrefying filth is needed to make the filth operate in predisposing the system to or determining an attack of either disease. This *something else*, the nature of which is still undetermined, but which appears to be closely, if not inseparably, connected with the discharges of the sick of the diseases, is denominated, for convenience sake, *specific.*

The general doctrine of *diarrhœal diseases*, in all their forms, is thus set forth by John Simon :—

" Nothing in medicine is more certain than the general meaning of high diarrhœal death-rates. The mucous membrane of the intestinal canal is the excreting surface to which nature directs all the accidental putridities which enter us. Whether they have been breathed or drunk or eaten, or sucked up into the blood from the surfaces of foul sores, or directly injected into blood-vessels by physiological experiments, there it is they settle and act. As wine 'gets into the head,' so these agents get into the bowels. There, as the universal result, they tend to produce diarrhœa—simple diarrhœa in the absence of specific infections; specific diarrhœa when the ferments of cholera and typhoid fever are in operation. And any such [irregular] distribution of diarrhœal disease as has just been noticed warrants a presumption—indeed, so far as I know, a practical certainty —that *in the districts which suffer high diarrhœal death-rates, the population either breathes or drinks a large amount of putrefying animal refuse.*" *

Diarrhœal disease (inclusive of common diarrhœa, simple cholera, and dysentery, but exclusive of malignant cholera and enteric fever) caused in England during the ten years 1861–70 not less than 215,823 deaths, and its local prevalence, measured by mortality, ranged from 57 (per 100,000 living) in the least unhealthy parts of the country to 195 (Yarmouth), 205 (Birmingham), and 299 (Liverpool).

* 'Papers relating to the Sanitary State of the People of England,' p. xi.

The remaining four classes of causes of premature death do not call for much detailed remark. Of Class VIII., *accidents*, *homicide*, and *suicide*, it is necessary to observe that much fatal accident is still a result of heedlessness and recklessness, not always on the part of the sufferer, but upon the part of those who are morally responsible for his safeguard when placed in circumstances involving danger to life by mechanical means. Since the legislation providing for the fencing of certain forms of machinery in manufactories, the loss of life by accident in these factories, at one time so formidable, has been very largely obviated.

The mortality from *homicide* has fluctuated but slightly, and from *suicide* has been almost stationary in the kingdom generally during the last fifteen or twenty years. But neither homicide nor suicide is a fixed quantity in a community, as Buckle would have it. The very small amount of fluctuation exhibited by deaths from suicide, as also from murder, in settled countries, within limited periods, was the stumbling-block over which Buckle fell so hopelessly and needlessly in the initial argument of his 'History of Civilization.'

Of Class IX., *Diseases of the Urinary Organs*, the conditions are too complex, and, as yet, too imperfectly known to admit of summary description. Of Class X., *Joint Disease*, a considerable proportion of instances must be referred to scrofulous (tubercular) disease ; and, finally, Class XI., *Skin Diseases*—this class includes abscess, both in its acute form, as it affects the cutaneous tissues (phlegmon), and in its chronic form, as it affects the same tissues, and is not uncommonly a variety of scrofulous disease.   Fatal skin disease, except probably as a con- comitant or result of scrofulous, syphilitic, or cancerous disease, is very rare.

If now we endeavour to bring together, in one con- nected view, the different conditions under which the numerous causes of premature death operate, supplying for this purpose such missing links in our detailed account as may be necessary, we shall find that, notwithstanding the great variety of causes as indicated by the large num- ber of names of fatal diseases, these conditions admit of arrangement into three broad categories, namely, (1) as relates to the individual ; (2) as relates to his nourishment and habits ; (3) as relates to his surroundings.

(1) *Conditions relating to the Individual.* — Notwith- standing the brevity of the references which have been made to inherited vices of the body, it must have been obvious from these how immeasurably an important part these vices play in fostering premature death.   Now, let it be clearly understood that in the different bodily vices to which attention has been directed—those degenera-

tions of race which are still so largely observed among all classes of the community, but more especially and markedly among some of our mining, manufacturing, and agricultural populations — we are witnessing the effects continued through generations, and exaggerated with each generation, of unwholesome conditions of life, which still exist and are still actively operating among us. Very much of the fatal influence of these inherited vices of constitution are hidden under the names of the assigned causes of death. The medical man is called upon to register as the cause of death the more immediate morbid conditions giving rise to death, not the remoter. But very commonly the immediate conditions are but an acci- dental or casual indication of the remoter condition, the inherited vice of constitution. As it is, however, under the terms " atrophy and debility," " scrofula," " premature birth," " teething," " convulsions," numerous deaths of infants are recorded who have been born immature ; and these constitute but a portion of deaths which originate in the immaturity and defective viability of the infant, hidden under other names. The liability to give birth to immature and non-viable children is one of the most marked characteristics of degenerated races. But the children born of these races who escape the perils of infancy are too apt to carry with them into later life the impress of their origin, with its proclivities to certain forms of fatal disease, and to succumb to affections which, although designated by some names indicative of local mischief, are in reality manifestations of an original vice of constitution. Hence, the propagation of these degenerated races holds a foremost place among the conditions which promote premature death.

(2) *Conditions relating to nourishment and habits.—* "Privation," here used in the sense of *starvation*, has a place among the causes of death. Thus, 82 deaths on the average were assigned annually to this cause during the 10 years 1866–75. Privation, moreover, plays an important part, as has been pointed out, in the development of typhus and of relapsing fever. But the less obvious results of privation enact even a more important part in promoting premature death than is shown by the instances cited. Privation, as destitution, is one of the most active agencies concerned in bringing about degeneration of race. It is, also, a most potent direct source of infantile mortality. Further, it exercises a powerful influence over the course of numerous diseases diminishing the chances of recovery from these, or accelerating their fatal consequences. In various modified forms, moreover, it tells evilly on the health-condition of large sections of the population—sections even which may not be subjected to the actual pinch of poverty. Particularly in infancy and childhood the privation resulting from neglect

and bad management, from insufficient or improper feeding, is the great source of rickets—the *English disease*,
as it has been designated by foreign writers, from its
believed especial prevalence in this country. Scurvy,
happily now very rare as a fatal disease in this kingdom, is
a modified form of privation ; so also is "purples." Other
modified forms, of great practical importance, are brought
about by the practice of adulteration or falsification of
articles of food, which not very long ago existed so largely,
and which is still not extinct. The recognition of these
different forms of privation becomes an important element
in the medical man's efforts to obviate the fatal consequences of certain diseases.

Then the habits of indulging in alcoholic liquors or
narcotic herbs exercises a supremely momentous influence
in the promotion of premature death. ."*Alcoholism*" is
credited with ten times as many deaths as "privation"
in the Registrar-General's returns. Thus, an average
number of 800 deaths were assigned annually to this
cause during the ten years 1866–75 ; but of alcoholism
as a cause of degeneration of race (with all its consequences), as a cause of numerous fatal diseases of the
digestive and urinary organs, as sapping in innumerable
ways the sources of life, with or without the help of
an excessive use of tobacco and of opium, who can tell
the whole story ?

5

But while the excessive use of intoxicating liquors must be ranked with destitution in all its forms as a condition promoting premature death, it must not be forgotten that if, on the one hand, it is one of the most formidable causes of degeneration of race, on the other hand degeneration of race is one of the most potent sources of the passion for intoxicating drink. Moreover, if, again, the excessive use of intoxicating drink is a fertile source of destitution, destitution itself, on the other hand, promotes such excessive use.

3. *Conditions relating to the Individual's surroundings.*— These conditions mainly concern the air he breathes, the water he drinks, and the soil he lives upon.

(*a*) *The Air.*—This is fouled in various manners, each manner contributing, and some in a particular fashion, to the fouling. The houses we live in, from their construction or from the way in which we occupy them, are too often principal sources of pollution of the air we breathe. They may be insufficiently lighted, or insufficiently provided with means for the inlet and outlet of fresh air, and so contribute relatively or directly to overcrowding. They may be imperfectly drained and unfurnished with means for the safe disposal of excremental or other filth, so that the air within them is laden with the products of putrefying organic matter, which the drains and depositories of filth failing of their proper functions, retain in and about them. To so large an extent does this pollution of the air of dwellings prevail—a pollution, as we have seen, which is concerned in the production of some of the most widely fatal diseases causing premature death, to wit, phthisis, malignant cholera, simple cholera, enteric fever, diarrhœa, dysentery, &c.—that we have it stated on official authority as follows :—

" There are houses, there are groups of houses, there are whole villages, there are considerable sections of towns, there are even entire and not small towns, where general slovenliness in everything which relates to the removal of refuse-matters—slovenliness which, in very many cases, amounts to utter bestiality of neglect, as local habit ; where within or just outside each house, or in spaces common to many houses, lies. for an indefinite time, undergoing fetid decomposition, more or less of the putrefiable refuse which house-life, and some sorts of trade-life, produce : excrement of man and brute, and garbage of all sorts, and ponded slop-waters : sometimes lying bare on the common surface ; sometimes unintentionally stored out of sight and recollection in drains or sewers which cannot carry them away ; sometimes held in receptacles specially provided to favour accumulation, as privy-pits and other cesspools for excrement and slop-water, and so-called dust-bins receiving kitchen-refuse and other filth. And with this state of things, be it on large or on small scale, two chief sorts of danger arise : one, that volatile effluvia from the refuse pollute the surrounding air and everything which it contains ; the other, that the liquid parts of the refuse pass by soakage or leakage into the surrounding soil, to mingle there, of course, in whatever water the soil yields, and in certain cases thus to occasion deadliest pollution of wells and springs. To a really immense extent, to an extent indeed which persons unpractised in sanitary inspection could scarcely find themselves able to imagine, dangers of these two sorts are prevailing throughout the length and breadth of this country, not only in their slighter degrees, but in degrees which are gross and scandalous, and very often, I repeat, truly bestial." *

As to occupation of houses : overcrowding of families therein, and the pollution of air thence arising, is an evil of very wide prevalence, giving occasion on the one hand to large development of fatal lung-disease, tubercular or other ; and on the other contributing to—in some cases determining—the existence of typhus, and under all circumstances favouring the spread and fatality of the infectious diseases.

* John Simon : 'Supplementary Report of Medical Officer of Privy Council and Local Government Board, 1874,' p. 15. New Series, No. II.

Then there are the air-pollutions occurring in work-shops in the pursuit of the different trades mentioned in a previous section, and which exercise so marked an influence in causing local excesses of prevalence of lung-disease.

(*b*) *Water.*—The most hurtful source of the pollution of water—the soakage or passage into wells and springs of decomposing organic refuse, and particularly putrefying excrement, has been noted in the previous section on Air. In so far as water is an important agency in promoting premature death, this for the most part depends upon its pollution with putrefying organic refuse, and especially excremental filth. Sicknesses arising from certain excesses of mineral matters in water do not appear, as a rule, to exercise in this country a marked influence in the promotion of premature death. The influence of water polluted with putrefying organic filth is seen in the production by it of fatal diarrhœa and dysentery, and in the propagation of enteric fever and malignant cholera. There is something inexpressibly revolting in the notion of persons and communities drinking water mingled with their own excrement, and yet it is one of the commonest facts of every-day life in this country ; and in addition, as we now know, excrement-polluted water is not rarely given to our infants and young children mingled with the milk on which they are fed.

(c) *Soil.*—The part of the soil in the promotion of premature death is as a source of pollution of the air we breathe and of the water we drink. The soil is the great laboratory in which the great mass of solid and liquid filth of those who live upon it undergoes its final decomposition and resolution into harmless elements. But when this soil becomes surcharged with filth its wholesome action ceases, and the changes which the filth undergoes within it commonly stop short at a period when its products are harmful to those living upon it. These products are taken up by the water in the soil and carried into the springs and wells, and they are also given off into the air above the soil by the movements of the air within the soil outwards, as it is influenced by the varying level of the sub-soil water, by variations of pressure in the atmosphere, and by other circumstances which go to bring about the breathing, so to say, of the sub-soil.

The atmosphere in its general aspects must be included among the surroundings of the individual active in some of their phases as a source of disease. But this action as represented in vicissitudes of weather and its relations to season may be regarded as uniform in its operation over large districts or over an entire country; and until the operation of locally existing fostering causes of fatal disease can be eliminated we shall be unable to discriminate the precise part which atmospheric changes play among the conditions under which the causes of premature death operate.

CHAPTER IV.

THE PREVENTION OF PREMATURE DEATH.

ENTERING now upon the subject of the *prevention of premature death*, two principal questions, in view of what has gone before, present themselves for consideration in this relation, namely :—

First, there is the question of dealing with, in order to their avoidance, the conditions under which the causes of premature death operate, which have been bequeathed to us ; and

Secondly, there is the question of dealing with the conditions which, as dealt with, would inevitably repeat, multiply at every stage, and perpetuate the first-named conditions.

A clear apprehension of the bearing of these questions is necessary to a right estimate of the subject now under consideration.

I. By far the greater proportion of the local conditions

which have been enumerated as fostering premature death is a legacy from previous generations. Thus the greater number of our towns and villages were built in times when sanitary knowledge did not exist as now understood, and the arrangement of their streets and houses, as well as the construction of the latter, were governed by local prejudices and individual views of comfort and utility, irrespective of considerations of wholesomeness. Hence, in the majority of cases, towns and villages became, and too commonly remain, mere conglomerations of houses, huddled together with no defined relations to each other except contiguity, and no bond of relationship except the thoroughfares about which they stand—thoroughfares, in the first instance, for the most part high-roads, and lanes, and bridle-paths, usually narrow, and never in their width having any certain relation to the height of the buildings erected along them. In rear of these thoroughfares, often accessible only through narrow tunnels which pierced the taller screen of houses running along the thoroughfare, as may still be seen in a great number of places, were crowded together the cottages of the poorer classes in close courts and narrow alleys—alleys frequently so narrow that a tall man could stretch his arms from side to side ; and the construction of the houses and their appurtenances too generally befitted the manner of their

arrangement. Contracted rooms of low ceiling, ill
lighted, and without any than accidental provision for the
movement of air in them were the rule. Indeed, as to
lighting, the law within living memory helped to exaggerate the evil of insufficiency in this respect by the
imposition of a window-tax. Further, the rule was for
all domestic filth, of every sort, to be deposited in or
about the house, within deep cesspools sunk beneath the
house or great receptacles outside, often of the capacity
of the largest room of the house ; while, sunk promiscuously in the soil upon and within which these great
reservoirs of filth existed, their liquid contents soaking
into it, were the wells from which the water for domestic
use was obtained.

Town, and village, and house-arrangements of this sort
may still be studied at large in every. part of the kingdom, for the most part bequeathed to us by our prede-
cessors of the age of sanitary ignorance. We say, "for the
most part," as it is well to know that the traditional habit
and practice of building in the manner described still
obtain in some districts of the kingdom uncontrolled.
Nor must we affect surprise at this. Thirty years only
have elapsed since it became possible to frame and give
force to the first comprehensive law of sanitary administration in England—the Public Health Act of 1848.

Now, these bequeathed conditions of unwholesomeness

are too often of a sort beyond reach of palliation. The brick-and-mortar jungles of our great towns, the peasant's cottage in numerous agricultural districts, the Northumbrian miner's cottage of old type, and the Welsh cottage also of old type, are utterly beyond the reach of true sanitary amendment. There is but one way of dealing with habitations of the kind here referred to, and that is by *destruction*. An important step has been made in this direction by the Legislature in the passing of the " Artizan and Labourers' Dwelling Act, of 1868," and the " Labourers' Dwellings Improvement Act, 1875." These important Acts provide that the sanitary authorities of town districts may, in a manner provided by the Acts, cause houses unfit for habitation to be amended as they require, or demolished, or may themselves acquire these houses, with a view to their demolition, and the construction upon their site of better houses and thoroughfares. Under the provisions of these Acts several sanitary authorities have already taken steps for the acquirement and demolition of old houses in parts of their towns which have defied all remedy and prove veritable plague-spots, and for laying out the cleared spots for thoroughfares and houses built according to modern notions.*

* Before the passing of the Acts referred to some large towns had begun a like course of improvement under the power of Local Acts of Parliament obtained for the purpose.

The importance of the principle involved in the Acts of Parliament above referred to cannot well be over-rated, for it strikes at the root of the greatest difficulty experienced in the sanitary reformation of our older towns. It is unfortunate, however, that the operation of this principle is as yet limited to town districts, for it would hardly be less beneficial in its application to many country districts.

The sections of the population exhibiting degeneration, as described in a previous chapter, must also be regarded as part of the bequeathed conditions which foster premature death; and the members of these sections who, by reason of the extent of degeneration manifested by them, whether as shown in disablement of body or of mind, form a large body of permanently destitute persons, come within the category. Indeed, much of the destitution which exists is to be regarded as a legacy from previous generations, occurring, as it does, among a class of the population which by successive deteriorations have reached a state of physical and mental incapacity which unfits them from earning at the best more than a bare subsistence, or which, as previously stated, renders them permanently destitute. Destitution is here, then, considered as one of the results of a preceding condition of things, of which the consequences, so far as those relate to habitation and the ordinary surroundings of life, have been described in the previous paragraphs. In the organised measures for the relief of destitution which now exist under the Poor Laws, we have, then, one of the most powerful means for arresting the further progress of degeneration in this direction.

Let it be observed of the first question here considered, that it relates to conditions for which the present time is not responsible ; which we have had bequeathed to us by our forefathers ; of which we are reaping the evil results sanitarily ; which have to be dealt with specially; and which wherever so dealt with must necessarily largely anticipate the measures for obviating the conditions fostering premature death which enter into the second question.

II. We come now to a consideration of the conditions fostering premature death which belong to the second question stated. These are conditions of every-day life which, undealt with, perpetuate the semi-barbaric stage of civilisation in its health-aspects, and, to be successfully dealt with, need continuous every-day attention. They are of two sorts, the one relating to the *individual* alone, the other to the individual in relation to others—in short, to the *community*. This primer does not concern itself with the individual, except incidentally. Other primers will be devoted to the personal care of health of the individual, as it is affected by his immediate surroundings. The present primer is limited to his relations as a member of a community; and it is necessary that the reasons for this distinction should be understood.

In dealing with the personal care of health, it has become customary to treat of man as if he were an abstract personage, capable of procuring for himself, and doing for himself all that was necessary for the maintenance of his corporeal and mental well-being; he is taught the qualities of good and of bad air, of good and of bad water, of the requirements of wholesome houses, of the characteristics of healthful food, of the due regulation of exercise and habits. He is taught all these things, not as vague generalities, but as matters of precise knowledge which involve a high degree of moral responsibility in their application. All this is an essential part in the great process of health-education now going on, and is producing excellent and progressively increasing results throughout the kingdom. But this teaching has been, and is still, too much dissociated from the actual facts of the circumstances under which man lives in a civilised country. The vast majority of individuals in England are dependent for the sort of air they breathe, the water they drink, the homes they inhabit, the food they consume, the opportunities of relaxation they may have, and even of the habits they form, upon others, and they can bring to bear but an infinitesimal influence over these all-important elements of their physical welfare. How many of us can exercise the slightest control over the qualities of the water we drink, or of the air we breathe, the construction of the houses we inhabit, the quality of the food we have to eat, or our physical habits? We are, for the most part, the slaves of our purse and our occupation, and unable to help ourselves in these matters, *except as we act together as a community.* It is at this point where our ordinary health-teaching mainly fails, namely, in *neglecting to show the circumstances under which individuals can only obtain sanitary essentials by conjoint action, as a community, and to what extent and in what matters the Legislature has made provision for such conjoint action.* The chief impediment to sanitary progress in England at this moment is the want of a just knowledge of the relations of the *community* to sanitary work, and the consequent misapprehensions of individuals and the insensitiveness of communities on this subject. What is now mainly wanted in England, in view of the furtherance of sanitary work, is an acuter sense among individuals generally of their common rights and common powers in sanitary matters.

Here, then, leaving the personal question for other primers of this series, it is proposed to indicate the provision which the law has made for the prevention or avoidance of those fostering conditions of premature death which come within our second question, the conditions of every-day life. `We shall deal with these in the order in which they have been summarised in Chapter III. (p. 19), first touching upon *privation*, and then in succession upon *alcoholism*, upon *air*, *water*, and *soil*, in their sanitary relations, including the consideration of the *home* and the *workshop*, and the *conditions of work;* and finally, the question of *infectious diseases* will be dealt with.

1. *Privation as destitution*, as we have endeavoured to show, is one of the most potent elements in the promotion of premature death ; and the administration of poor's. relief, as it obtains in this country, has a sanitary aspect of the greatest moment. This has now been recognised for England and Ireland (as previously in Scotland*), by the Legislature, in the recent amalgamation of the Central Authority for Poor-law Administration, and the former Central Authorities for Public Health Administration in one body, termed the Local Government Board. This new Government Department, formed in England in 1871 (Local Government Board Act, 1871), was

---

* "The Board of Supervision for the Relief of the Poor and of Public Health" is the designation of the corresponding Central Authority in Scotland.

especially designed to give unity of action in the administration of Poor-law and of Sanitary-law in such matters, when the two sorts of law overlapped, and, rightly applied, would add to the efficiency—indeed, were necessary to the efficiency—of each other. Hitherto this great design has not proved as effective in operation as was hoped for, and the important object aimed at by the amalgamation has been largely frustrated. This seems to have arisen from difficulties of departmental working, rather than from any error in the principle ; but notwithstanding this failure, it is a great gain to have legislative recognition of the essentially sanitary aspect of some of the phases of poor-relief.

In so far as privation, in its less recognised forms, may arise from the unwholesome preparation, the fraudulent sophistication, or the improper state for consumption of articles of food, the Legislature has not been unmindful of the needs of communities. The Bake-house Regulation Act of 1863 provides for the due regulation and proper cleanliness of bake-houses, and for the obviation of those numerous causes which at one time tended to render the bread made in them filthy and unwholesome. The Sale of Food and Drugs' Act, 1875, provides an important machinery for detecting adulterations of articles of food and drugs, and for the punishment of adulterators. Finally, the Public Health Act, 1875, provides that a medical officer of health, or inspector of nuisances, may inspect any animal, carcase, meat, poultry, game, flesh, fish, fruit, vegetables, corn, bread, flour, or milk, exposed for sale, and seize the same, if any of such articles appear to him diseased, unsound, unwholesome, or unfit for the food of man. The Act also provides for the punishment, by fine or imprisonment, of any person exposing articles in the condition named for sale.

The three Acts of Parliament here referred to give very large powers for dealing with sophistications of articles of food injurious to health, if they be duly administered.

2. *Alcoholism.*—The excessive use of intoxicating liquors as a fostering condition of premature death is one of the most difficult questions in social administration. By the Public-House Closing Act of 1864, which regulates the hours of closing of inns, public-houses, and places of refreshment where intoxicating drinks are sold, an attempt is made to control, after a minute fashion, public drinking; but it must be confessed that the most obvious agency in controlling habits of drinking is the direct action of the police and the punishment inflicted by magistrates for drunkenness. The question of dealing with the excessive use of intoxicating liquors is, however, at the root a moral one, and must ultimately rest mainly with the pulpit. But in so far as this excessive use is a result

6

of the degraded condition in which large masses of our labouring populations live, and of a craving which is one of the most significant indications of the mental and physical deterioration which we have described in a previous section, the abatement of the excessive use of intoxicating liquors will only follow, step by step, upon the removal of these conditions. There are localities where such abatement has followed concurrently with great improvements in the physical conditions under which the people live. It may be that these localities are as yet too few to have affected markedly the general prevalence of drunkenness in the kingdom; but they surely show that a primary element in the prevention of the excessive use of intoxicating liquors is the amelioration of the sanitary state of the population.

3. *The Air in its relations to the Home, the Workshop, and the Community.*—The air we breathe, with reference to its purity, requires to be considered in relation to the house we live in, the places we work in, and, incidentally, the conditions of that work, and to the community of which we form a part. The law makes large provision, in aid of individual action, to secure purity of air under the several circumstances mentioned. This provision takes two forms. The one form is directed to the immediate obviation of conditions which pollute the air in various

ways injurious to health, and to the prevention of their recurrence—the removal of *nuisances*, in short. The other form is directed to secure such structural arrangements of houses and groups of houses as will obtain for them the essential conditions of wholesomeness, and will prevent the repetition of those traditional modes of building which have proved the most formidable obstacles to sanitary improvement. These provisions are made in the Public Health Act, 1875; in which Act have been consolidated the various sanitary Acts passed by the Legislature since 1848, including the Public Health Act of that year. In addition, factories, work-shops, and work-places are regulated by several special Acts of Parliament.

Nuisances.—Under the Public Health Act, 1875, a nuisance is declared to be—

(*a*) Any premises in such a state as to be a nuisance or injurious to health ;

(*b*) Any pool, ditch, gutter, water-course, privy, urinal, cesspool, drain, or ashpit so foul or in such a state as to be a nuisance or injurious to public health ;

(*c*) Any animal so kept as to be a nuisance or in- jurious to health ;

(*d*) Any accumulation or deposit which is a nuisance or injurious to health ;

(*e*) Any house, or part of a house, so overcrowded as to be dangerous or injurious to the health of the inmates, whether or not members of the same family;

(*f*) Any factory, workshop, or workplace (not already under the operation of any general Act for the regulation of factories or bakehouses) not kept in a cleanly state, or not ventilated in such a manner as to render harmless as far as practicable, any gases, vapours, dust, or other impurities generated in the course of the work carried on therein that are a nuisance or injurious to health, or so overcrowded while work is carried on as to be dangerous or injurious to the health of those employed therein ;

(*g*) Any fire-place or furnace which does not as far as practicable consume the smoke arising from the combustibles used therein, and which is used for working engines by steam, or in any mill, factory, dye-house, brewery, bake-house, or gaswork, or in any manufacturing or trade process whatsoever ; and

(*h*) Any chimney (not being the chimney of a private dwelling-house) sending forth black smoke in such quantity as to be a nuisance, shall be deemed to be nuisances liable to be dealt with summarily in manner provided by the Act.

Overcrowding, moreover, as it is liable to appear in lodging-houses, common and other, is dealt with by special provisos of the Act, as well as by the Common Lodging-House Acts. Offensive accumulations for trade purposes, if reasonable care be taken to obviate annoy- ance from them, and they be not unduly kept, are exempt from the above provisions.

Here, then, there is large provision made by the law for dealing with sources of air-fouling injurious to health which are connected with the ordinary current events of every-day life.

Moreover, in view of a systematic prevention of cer- tain nuisances, sanitary authorities may undertake them- selves, or frame bye-laws imposing such duty upon the householder for the cleansing at proper intervals of the footways and pavements adjoining any premises, and for the removal of filth of all sorts from premises ; also for the prevention of nuisances from filth, and for the regula- tion of the keeping of animals so as not to become a nuisance.

Houses.—If now we turn to the structural conditions of houses, we find no lack of provisions made for securing and maintaining their healthfulness. The same Act of Parliament from which we have just quoted gives powers to sanitary authorities to frame bye-laws as to houses with respect

(a) To the construction of walls, foundations, roofs, and chimneys of new buildings, for securing stability and the prevention of fires, and for purposes of health ;

(b) To the sufficiency of the space about buildings to secure a· free circulation of air, and with respect to the ventilation of buildings ; and

(c) To the drainage of buildings, to water-closets, earth-closets, privies, ash-pits, and cesspools in connection with buildings, and to the closing of buildings or parts of buildings unfit for human habitation, and to prohibition of their use for such habitation.

A series of model bye-laws have recently been published by the Local Government Board to give effect to these provisions. These bye-laws show how large is the power put into the hands of communities for obviating the more serious sources of unhealthiness which have hitherto too commonly attached to houses as ordinarily constructed and arranged. Duly carried into effect, these bye-laws would effectually prevent (unless there be overcrowding, which, as we have seen, is otherwise provided for) injurious fouling of the air within, and about houses from the imperfect means of ventilation and lighting, from bad drainage, and from the improper provision for the disposal of domestic refuse and filth.

Unfortunately these provisions for securing from the beginning the fitness for occupation of a house, as fitness is now understood, do not apply everywhere in the kingdom. Their operation is restricted to town districts— *urban* districts, properly so called. There is no place where a new house is erected, where these provisions, modified according to circumstances, are not needed. The evils of imperfectly constructed and arranged houses are universal, and the means to prevent ill-construction and arrangement should be universal also.

The Workshop and Work-place.—In addition to the provision for the ventilation of workshops and against their overcrowding contained in the Public Health Act, 1875, several Acts of Parliament exist for regulating the conditions under which particular trades are pursued. These Acts relate to the general sanitary condition of the factories and workshops to which they refer, the safety of the individuals employed from accidents liable to be caused by machinery, the duration of the occupation of children and young people, the time to be given for their meals and the places for eating them, the days to be set apart as holidays and half-holidays, the education of the children employed, and the fitness of the children for employment. The special provisions of the Acts include the cleanliness of workshops and the means of ventilation, particularly in cases where the manufacture carried on in them produces much dust or otherwise injuriously fouls the air. Very important restrictions are placed upon the employ- ment of children or young persons, or both, in trades directly injurious to health, such as the processes of silver- ing mirrors or making white lead, metal grinding or the dipping of lucifer matches, and in certain trades in- volving night work. The provisions, indeed, of the Factories and Workshops Acts touch the core of some of the most important sources of physical degeneration in the kingdom, and put under control the most formidable of the conditions, which, as we have seen in a previous section, contribute to produce excessive prevalence of lung-disease, including phthisis, in various localities. The provisions of the Coal Mine and Metalliferous Mine Regulation Acts do the same for workers in mines, as far as this is practicable.

The Community.—Every district has its local authority empowered to administer within it the sanitary laws, and among these laws ample provision is made for dealing with the sanitary requirements not of houses only, or of workshops and work-places only, but also of the com- munity as a whole. Although if every house and workshop were made free from unwholesome conditions, the aggregation of which they form a part would be equally free, such freedom cannot be accomplished with respect to the commoner conditions of nuisance except by the community acting as a body. The drainage of the houses requires a common system of sewerage for its efficiency; and general cleanliness and the regulation of thorough-fares, or of markets, or slaughter-houses, and the prevention of unwholesome conditions therein, also the regulation of offensive businesses, is possible only on condition of the community as a whole undertaking, through its representatives, the several duties. The Public Health Act, 1875, provides for the community, as represented by its sanitary authorities, carrying out the duties referred to. It may construct sewers, govern thorough-fares, perform all general acts of cleansing required, and by means of bye-laws subject markets, slaughter-houses, and offensive trades to sanitary regulations.

Water.—A community has not less power in supplementing individual action in respect to water than it has with respect to house-construction, drainage, sewerage, and the abatement of nuisances, trade or other. A sanitary authority, under the Public Health Act, 1875, has large powers of providing water for its district, protecting such water from pollution, or closing polluted supplies. This power may be exercised either in procuring a general supply or in developing and guarding particular supplies from wells, springs, &c.

The Soil.—The sanitary law in this respect is still defective. It does not contain express provisions which would secure proper drainage of the soil, or which would prohibit the erection of dwelling-houses upon soils, such as the made earths produced by the deposits of domestic refuse of all kinds from towns, which are unfit to form sites. Such drainage and purification as a soil may receive from the agency of a sanitary authority is usually incidental to the laying down of sewers, the cleansing of the surface, the removal of domestic refuse, and the prevention, under certain conditions, of the deposit of such refuse in cesspits and privy-pits. In view of what we have said as to dampness of soil being a condition of phthisis, it would seem that special provisions for the drainage of the sub-soil, and furthermore for the prevention of building upon accumulations of town refuse or organic refuse of any sort are needed.

Infectious Diseases.—Infectious diseases, by reason of their infectiousness, require separate consideration in reference to their prevention. In so far as their prevalence may be affected by overcrowding, by conditions of uncleanliness of habitation, by nuisances from accumulations of filth, by improper drainage and sewerage, or by

polluted water or soil, the different provisions of the
sanitary laws which have been referred to in previous
paragraphs meet them more or less completely.   But it
is practicable to deal with some infections independently
of the conditions which may favour their action.   In this
respect small-pox stands alone among the several infectious disorders.   In vaccination we possess an *absolute*
preventive of this disease, if we were to use it properly;
but in other infectious diseases we are restricted in our
efforts of direct prevention to the isolation of cases.
Isolation is also an important means of dealing with
small-pox when present among a community; but while
it is the sole means with which we can effectively combat
scarlet-fever, diphtheria, typhus, &c., with respect to
small-pox we possess a surer preventive agent in
vaccination.

The public provision for vaccination, under the Vaccination Acts of 1867 and 1871, is the most complete of
all our measures of sanitary law, and when it shall have
come into such operation as to affect several generations
of young children and the accumulations of unvaccinated
and imperfectly vaccinated persons in the kingdom, and
when the relics of years of prejudice, ignorance, indifference, and carelessness as to vaccination shall have
died out, small-pox will decline to an extent to which the
present existence of the disease among us, although a

trifle compared to its previous existence, will appear to be enormous. The arrangements for public vaccination provide (free of cost) for every child being compulsorily vaccinated—

(1) Before it is three months' old;
(2) Direct from the vesicle of a child already vaccinated;
(3) In at least four places, if vaccinated by puncture; or so as to give an equal amount of local disturbance if vaccinated otherwise.

There is little fear of a child who has been successfully vaccinated in this fashion ever afterwards contracting small-pox, unless under quite exceptional circumstances of exposure to the infection. But even this rare liability may be effectually extinguished *if every child be re-vaccinated on attaining puberty.* Re-vaccination is not compulsory, but public vaccinators are empowered to. revaccinate, free of cost, on application to them. Already the present arrangements for public vaccination in this kingdom have changed the incidence of small-pox attacks. Formerly the incidence was chiefly upon infants and young children; now the infants and young children born since 1867, unquestionably the best vaccinated persons in the kingdom, are escaping the disease, while its chief incidence is falling upon the children and persons who were born before the Acts now in force came into operation ; that is to say, among the worst vaccinated part of the community.

The prejudice entertained by some persons against vaccination is, in reality, the result of ignorance of small-pox. The diminution of small-pox in its severe forms since the introduction of vaccination has been such that comparatively few persons living are familiar with the disease and the horrible disfigurement it is apt to give rise to in the unvaccinated when not fatal. The evil being unfamiliar is undreaded, and the sure means of prevention undervalued or decried.

With respect to infectious diseases generally, the Public Health Act, 1875, provides that sanitary authorities may (a) erect and maintain hospitals for the isolation of the infectious sick ; empowers them (b) to remove, with a magistrate's order, and to institute proper means for removal, to such hospitals persons suffering from dangerous infectious sickness who have no proper lodging or accommodation, who lodge in rooms occupied by members of more than one family, or who are on board any ship or vessel; also (c) to destroy infected bedding; (d) to provide means for the disinfection of infected articles of bedding and clothing ; (e) to provide also a proper carriage for the conveyance of the infectious sick. The same Act also enables the sanitary authority (f) to cleanse and disinfect premises ;

(*g*) prohibits the exposure of infected persons or things, and (*h*) the letting of houses for lodgings in which infection has been without they have been certified as efficiently disinfected. The Act imposes, also, a penalty for giving false information of the existence of infectious diseases in houses let in lodgings. Further, sanitary authorities are empowered to erect mortuaries. Let it be added here, that urban sanitary authorities, under the Burials Acts, have also power to provide and regulate burial-grounds.

The several provisions of the Sanitary Laws which have been here enumerated would have been of little avail if no arrangements had been made to secure their execution. Although these laws are still to a regretable extent permissive only, not compulsory, still there are important parts of them which sanitary authorities are required to carry into effect, such as the search for and proceedings as to nuisance, failing which the Local Government Board can take proceedings against an authority for default of duty. Moreover, it is incumbent upon sanitary authorities to appoint officers to act—a medical officer of health and inspector of nuisances—for the investigation of the sanitary requirements of the district, and for taking the initiative in abating nuisances, and in proceedings for the general amelioration of its sanitary state and the limitation of disease.

This brief summary very imperfectly indicates the large provision made by the sanitary laws for the prevention of the various causes of premature death and to facilitate the action of individuals and of communities for the removal of the conditions under which these causes operate. ·It will have been observed, notwithstanding the brevity of the statement, how, with hardly an exception, the main conditions which have been described as concerned in the production of premature death are more or less closely provided for remedially in the various laws. These laws are still imperfect in many details, but they fairly express and contain the main principles of the sanitary reformation of the kingdom. Applied as they are now being applied, and notwithstanding much blundering and apathetic administration, they have effected incalculable benefits tending to the removal of sickness and the saving of life in many localities. That they are capable of affording wider and even greater benefits than have as yet been obtained from them cannot be gainsaid. Indeed, it may be asserted, that the whole power of the sanitary law for good is still very imperfectly understood. An averred inefficiency of the law often rests not so much in its imperfection as in the unintelligent way in which it is too commonly administered. And this imperfect administration is but the reflex of that insensitiveness and indifference which still so largely affects our communities in ordinary

times in sanitary matters. Great as has been the awaken-
ing of the public at large to the importance of sanitary
work in its relation to the welfare of families and of communities, it has not been such as to secure as yet that
lively and intelligent interest in the subject which is the
best security for continuous attention to it, and for successive improvements in sanitary law and administration.
Seeing what remains to be done, of which one aspect,
and the gravest, perhaps, is presented in the account
given in these pages of premature death as observed in
England, we are apt, perhaps, to underrate what has
been done. It is but thirty years ago (1848) since the
first comprehensive scheme of sanitary administration in
this country received the sanction of the Legislature, and
if it were not for the consciousness of how much remains
undone, we might regard with justifiable pride the
advances made in sanitary legislation, sanitary administration, and sanitary practice, within that brief period.
But while a solitary spot remains in England, which
would justify the accounts we have given of some of the
local conditions under which the causes of premature
death operate, it would be idle to boast of facts which,
in reality, are but a shadow of good things to come.

THE END.